An Alien in My House

by Shenaaz G. Nanji   illustrated by Chum McLeod

Second
Story
Press

One day Ben told his friends,

"An alien has invaded my house."

"An alien?" they asked. "From where?"

"Mars, stars, space — who knows?" said Ben.

"His face is covered with bike tracks. His body comes apart like Lego. He pulls out his teeth and says 'my pearlies.' He pulls off his hair and says 'my rug.' He walks on three legs, *rat-a-tap-tap*."

That day, the Alien told his friends, "I've moved into a monster's house."

"A monster?" they asked. "From where?"

"Park, jungle, zoo — who knows? His face is as smooth as butter. His body is stretchy like rubber. He twists into every letter of the alphabet. He even walks on his hands."

Ben said, "The Alien is as quiet as a thief! He dozes in the same old chair for hours. A button in his ear helps him understand our language. A puffer in his pocket helps him breathe our air. Without it, his chest squeaks like an orchestra of mice."

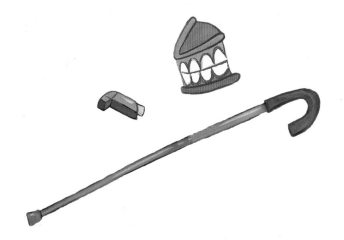

The Alien said, "The Monster yak-yaks like a parrot. He shouts and talks to his computer for hours. He has hidden springs in his feet. Up the stairs, down the banisters. Over the chair, under the table. Now I see him, now I don't."

"The computer in the Alien's head has crashed," said Ben. "He remembers my chores but forgets his promise of ice cream. His room is filled with bottles of pills and potions. And he only eats green food — peas, broccoli, spinach."

"Yuck. Don't eat that stuff," his friends warned. "You'll be green and slimy!"

"The wires in the Monster's head are crossed!" said the Alien. "He remembers my promise of ice cream but forgets his chores. His room is filled with rocks and stinky socks. And he eats only C food — candy, chocolate, cake and chips."

"Oof! Don't eat that stuff," his friends warned. "You'll puff up like a balloon!"

A few days later Ben's friends asked, "Did the Alien go back to space?"

"No," said Ben. "I, um, asked him to stay."

"You did *what*?" his friends shrieked. "You *want* him here?"

"Hey, we're best buddies now," said Ben. "On cold days he warms me with bear hugs and stories. He talks about the good old days when he was a soldier. He makes it sound like a movie. He even showed me his medals. The Alien's a hero!"

"When I had to go for soccer practice, my bike had a flat tire," Ben said. "The Alien gave me a ride in his Space Car."

"I wish the Alien lived with me," said his friends.

That day the Alien's friends asked, "Did you move out of the Monster's house yet?"

"No," said the Alien. "I, um, I'm going to stay."

"You are *what*?" his friends gasped. "You *want* to be there?"

"Yup, we're best buddies now," said the Alien. "On cold days, he brings me warm memories. And he taught me wrestling, soccer and hockey. I can kick, shoot, score — with a mouse that lives in his computer. The Monster's a genius!"

"When I had to go for bingo, I couldn't find my puffer. The Monster found it in a jiffy."

"I wish the Monster lived with me," said the Alien's friends.

The next day Ben announced, "I've made a discovery. It's huge."

"Cool," said his friends. "Tell us."

Ben giggled. "One day I'll be an Alien, too. Just like my Grandpa!"

That same day the Alien announced, "I have made a discovery. It's important."

"Splendid," said his friends. "Please tell us."

The Alien sighed. "Once I was a Monster, too. Just like my grandson, Ben."

Dedicated to the loving memory of my father, KAZA, and to all the
Alien Grandpas in the world.

My sincere thanks to everyone at Vermont College.

— S.G.N.

NATIONAL LIBRARY OF CANADA CATALOGUING IN PUBLICATION

Nanji, Shenaaz
An alien in my house / by Shenaaz Nanji ; illustrated by Chum McLeod.

ISBN 1-896764-77-0

I. McLeod, Chum II. Title.

PS8577.A573A84 2003   jC813'.54   C2003-904608-7

Edited by Charis Wahl
Designed by Laura McCurdy

Printed in Hong Kong

Second Story Press gratefully acknowledges the support of the Ontario Arts Council and the Canada
Council for the Arts for our publishing program. We acknowledge the financial support of the
Government of Canada through the Book Publishing Industry Development Program, and the
Government of Ontario through the Ontario Media Development Corporation's
Ontario Book Initiative.

Published by
SECOND STORY PRESS
720 Bathurst Street, Suite 301
Toronto, Ontario, Canada
M5S 2R4
www.secondstorypress.on.ca